Islam

Cameron

Seek reading to obtain understanding that you may share in wisdom

Peace

Forestlands

by Elizabeth Ring • Photographs by Dwight Kuhn

BLACKBIRCH PRESS
An imprint of Thomson Gale, a part of The Thomson Corporation

Detroit • New York • San Francisco • San Diego • New Haven, Conn. • Waterville, Maine • London • Munich

© 2005 Thomson Gale, a part of the Thomson Corporation.

Thomson and Star Logo are trademarks and Gale and Blackbirch Press are registered trademarks used herein under license.

For more information, contact
The Gale Group, Inc.
27500 Drake Rd.
Farmington Hills, MI 48331-3535
Or you can visit our Internet site at http://www.gale.com

ALL RIGHTS RESERVED
No part of this work covered by the copyright hereon may be reproduced or used in any form or by any means—graphic, electronic, or mechanical, including photocopying, recording, taping, Web distribution or information storage retrieval systems—without the written permission of the publisher.

Every effort has been made to trace the owners of copyrighted material.

Photo Credits: Cover, all photos © Dwight Kuhn Photography

LIBRARY OF CONGRESS CATALOGING-IN-PUBLICATION DATA

Ring, Elizabeth, 1920-
  Forestlands / by Elizabeth Ring.
    p. cm. — (Communities in nature)
  Includes bibliographical references and index.
  ISBN 1-4103-0319-5 (hardcover : alk. paper)
  1. Forest animals—Juvenile literature. 2. Forest plants—Juvenile literature. I. Title II. Series: Ring, Elizabeth, 1920- . Communities in nature.
  QL112.R558 2002
  578.73—dc22
                                                  2004010893

Printed in China
10 9 8 7 6 5 4 3 2 1

Introduction

From high in the air, one kind of forest looks a lot like another. But when you walk in the woods, you find out how different each woodland can be.

Each forest has its own kinds of trees. Where winters are short and mild, most forests are made up of broad-leafed (deciduous) trees. Farther north, where winters are longer and colder, cone-bearing (coniferous) evergreen trees mix in with the leafy trees. In the far north, where winters are longest and coldest, forests have only evergreen trees. Each forest has its own wildlife. Some animals and plants are at home in two, even three kinds of woods.

Leafy and evergreen trees grow in forestlands that cover valleys and mountains for miles.

In the Leafy Forest

It's almost always cool in the forest, even on hot summer days, and there's a sweet, woodsy smell all around. You're in the shade of tall trees, like maples, birches, and oaks. When the wind blows through the treetops, the branches sway. They wave their leaves slowly, this way and that, like arms waving big bunches of green flags. Sunlight comes down through the leaves and lies in patches on the path through the woods.

In deciduous forests, leafy trees make cool places for animals to live—and for us to visit.

I carry binoculars when my brother and I take walks in the woods. Field glasses make things look big and close to your face. One time, I saw a bird's nest up close—with two tiny chicks' heads sticking out. Then, a hummingbird landed on the nest's edge. Both chicks opened their beaks so wide it looked as if my finger could fit inside their mouths.

The trees are tall, and you need field glasses to see what is happening up in the branches.

My brother and I took turns watching the ruby-throated hummingbird feed its two hungry chicks. I had never seen a hummingbird sit so still. Usually, a hummingbird darts so fast you can't even see its wings beat. Sometimes, when it feeds on nectar, it just stays in one spot over a flower—like a little helicopter hanging there in the air.

There is a ruby-throated hummingbird on the edge of its nest, feeding its hungry chicks.

Another day, we saw a woodpecker feeding its chicks. It was a male pileated woodpecker, with a cap of red feathers sticking up from its head. You don't need binoculars to find this bird. You just follow its loud *rat-a-tat* hammer sound. It is pecking at tree bark to find hidden insects to eat—or maybe to hollow out a nest in a tree.

And over there is a pileated woodpecker poking insects into its chicks' open beaks.

Look at that moth with its lacy wings—
fluttering like a ballet dancer up on her toes.
I hope it won't be eaten by any bird. As it is,
the luna has only about seven days to live.
In that time, the female will mate and lay one
or two hundred brown eggs, maybe more.
Caterpillars will hatch, eat leaves, and grow
fat. They will make cocoons. Inside the
cocoon, they will turn into new lacy-winged
luna moths that will come out and dance—
for one short week.

Luna moths spend their short lives dancing their nights away, waving their lacy wings.

Red squirrels don't dance, but they are about the busiest animals in the woods. They run around all over the woods, picking up nuts, acorns, and seeds. They make up for their small size by being scrappy and bold. They stand still and scold at you. They're saying: "Don't you dare come too close." We don't.

Red squirrels scurry all over the woods looking for nuts, acorns, and seeds.

A porcupine won't scold at you the way a squirrel does! Porcupines don't have to be scrappy or bold. They wear stiff, sharp hairs called quills—all over themselves. Any enemy that grabs that slow, prickly animal gets quills stuck in its skin. Some people think porcupines shoot their quills out, as if they were arrows. That's not true, but you would never want to pick a porcupine up.

Porcupines waddle slowly around, protected from enemies by their prickly quills.

A gray tree frog's skin is as different from a porcupine's as it could be. The frog has no hair at all. It can climb trees without falling because it has sticky suction cups on its toes. And it can hide. Its colors can change from green to gray and back again. The frog sometimes looks just like part of a plant, a rock, or the ground.

Most mushrooms look like little umbrellas or flat plates. But a puffball mushroom looks like its name—a soft, puffy ball. When you poke a puffball, yellowish, smoky-looking puffs of dust burst out from a little hole in the pouch. The dust is made up of tiny, dry, powdery spores. Millions of spores float off through the air and plant themselves in damp places in the woods.

Opposite page: A gray tree frog is nearly invisible as it squats on a log among curly fungi plants.

Right: Puffball mushrooms puff out clouds of spores from their fat, ball-shaped pouches.

A rotting log would be a good place for a puffball spore to land. Many kinds of small plants—mushrooms, moss, lichens, and mold—feed on the log. Little animals live in and on logs, too. You can always find beetles, termites, and ants. They all break the wood down and help the log rot. Some day, the log will sink into the forest floor. Forest soil in the woods is so deep with old wood, dead leaves, and crumbled bones, you almost bounce when you walk.

Damp, rotting logs make good places for spores and seeds to settle on and grow.

A black bear will feed at a log in a big way, but it doesn't eat wood. It digs for the insects that live in the log. It scoops up beetles and ants with its strong claws and laps them up with its long tongue. Black bears also like to eat berries, acorns, and nuts. Bears do eat some mice and fish—but a black bear's favorite food is honey. It will tear open a honeybee hive even with bees swarming around. The bear's thick fur protects it from bee stings.

Black bears don't often chase people, deer, or any other large animal in the woods.

Black bears dig for beetles and ants in logs—if they can't find a beehive to raid.

A small, white-tailed deer fawn would probably be safe, because a black bear can't see very well. From a distance, a fawn's spotted coat might look to the bear like spots on a tree stump. Many animals hunt deer to eat. Deer eat only plants.

The spots on a deer fawn help to camouflage it in the sun-spotted woods.

About three weeks from the day we watched the hummingbird feed its chicks, we found only an empty nest. My brother climbed up the tree to get a close look. The nest was covered with lichen and lined with soft plant down and spider web silk. Where did the chicks go? Will they come back? We don't know. But my brother and I will come back to the woods—to see all the new sights we know will be here.

The tiny hummingbird nest sits empty after the chicks have flown off.

In the Mixed Forest

When I go into the woods, I see leafy and evergreen trees growing side by side. The top leaves of the tall, leafy oak and maple trees make a canopy, like a tent high over my head. I like to follow the stream that runs through the woods. The shadowy water is full of fish. They slip around rocks, sunken pinecones, and fallen trees.

Tall leafy and evergreen trees grow side by side in a mixed forest.

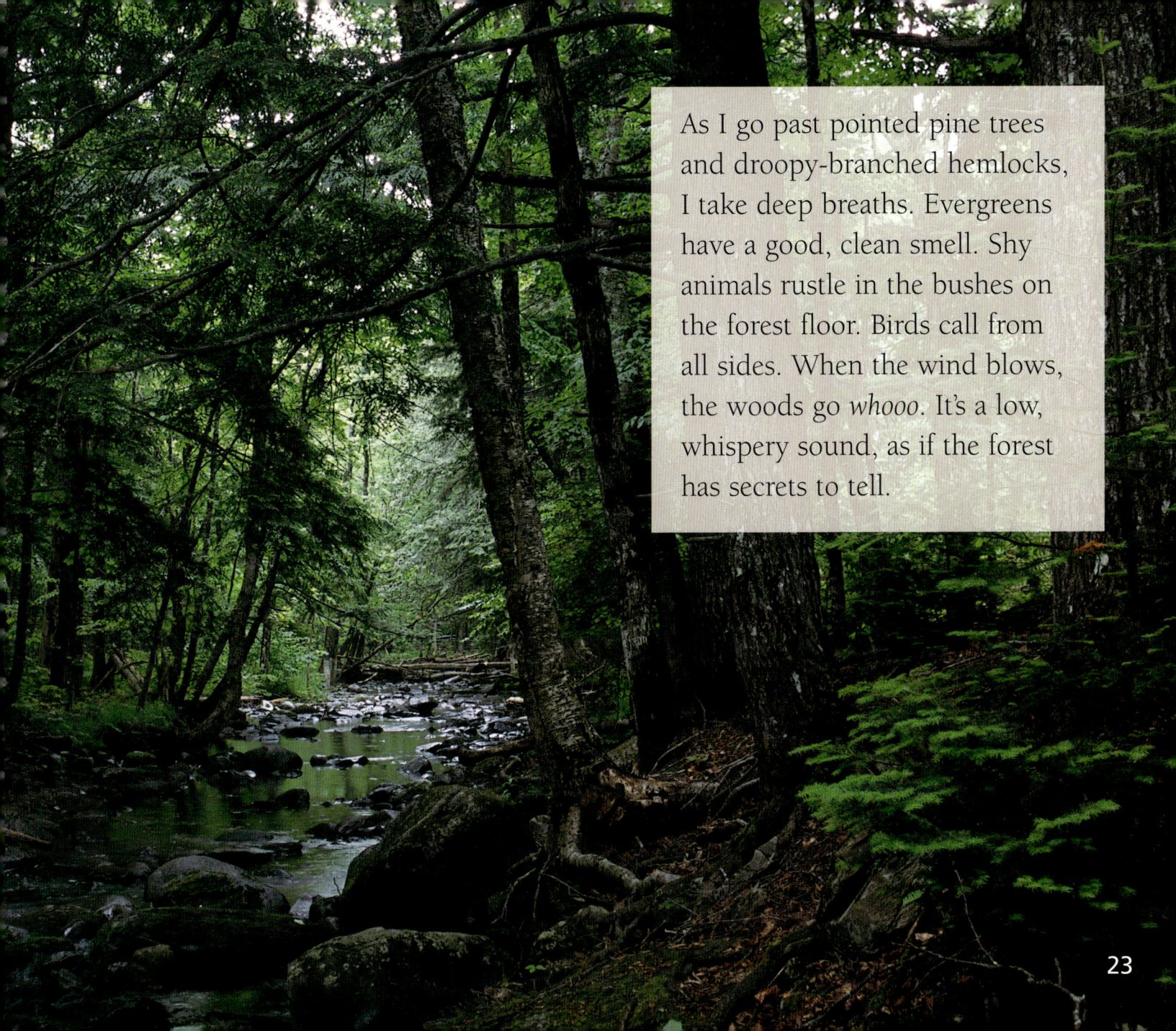

As I go past pointed pine trees and droopy-branched hemlocks, I take deep breaths. Evergreens have a good, clean smell. Shy animals rustle in the bushes on the forest floor. Birds call from all sides. When the wind blows, the woods go *whooo*. It's a low, whispery sound, as if the forest has secrets to tell.

Things change all year long in the woods. Trees topple down and become logs. Logs rot. Mushrooms grow right out of the dead wood. I find mushrooms as big as lunch plates and some as small as the end of my thumb. Wherever wood or the ground is damp or decayed, mushrooms can spring up—sometimes overnight, if it rains. They push up out of fungi that grow in the ground, in dead leaves, or underneath bark.

Big and small mushrooms sprout from the damp, dead wood of rotting logs.

A toad looks for shade beneath toadstools—even though stools are usully sat on.

One day, I saw a toad by some toadstools—a kind of mushroom you find in the woods. You might think a toad would sit on top of a toadstool. But this toad was on the ground. Just then, it flicked out its wide, sticky tongue and captured a fly from the air. Then, with one push of its springy hind feet, it jumped into a pond. Toads don't drink with their mouths. They soak water up—right through their skin—from wet moss or grass or by going for a swim.

All kinds of creatures hop, run, and crawl on the forest floor. Once, I watched a big female wolf spider creeping along on some green moss. Under her belly she carried a white sac of eggs. I wished I could be around to see her eggs hatch. Imagine watching fifty or maybe even two hundred tiny spiders scramble out of the sac and run around on their mother's back!

Female wolf spiders carry their eggs in white sacs under their bellies.

Many plants besides bushes and trees live on the forest floor. In the summer, I find flowers called lady's slippers in low places in the woods. The person who named them thought they look like showy shoes that ladies might wear. To me, the flowers look more like fat pink bees stuck on green stems. In some states, there are laws to keep people from taking them out of their natural homes and replanting them in their yards. Animals, though, pay no attention to laws—and deer, especially, like sweet lady's slippers to eat.

Showy lady's slippers blossom in shady places on the forest's dark floor.

You won't break any laws if you take home a few hemlock-tree cones. The cones on the trees hang tip-down from the ends of twigs. The fallen cones you take home are almost as hard as rocks and will last a long time.

The branches of some hemlocks swoop low. Sometimes, I like to sit under them and just listen to the woods' sounds.

Many hard, scaly cones hang from the branches of hemlock trees.

If I hear a bird that goes *k tsee-k tsee-k tsee* and *chip ee-chip ee-chip ee-chip* (well, something like that), I can tell it's a Nashville warbler's song. Once, I found a warbler's half-hidden nest on the ground. Three chicks were inside. Pretty soon, a parent—their mother or father, I couldn't tell which because they look just alike—flew to the nest and poked insects into the chicks' wide-open mouths.

A Nashville warbler brings insects to feed to its three open-mouthed chicks.

One afternoon, I noticed a saw-whet owl perched on a tree branch. It looked sound asleep, but it heard me, it seemed. It cocked its head toward where I stood. It puffed up its brown-and-white feathers. I think it was trying to make itself look bigger— maybe to scare me away. I slowly backed off, to let the owl get back to sleep. It would probably be hunting insects and mice a good bit of the night and would need all the sleep it could get.

A saw-whet owl sits on a stump, waiting for nightfall to hunt insects and mice.

If I hear a high, squeaky *chip-chip-chip-chip* or a *chuck-chuck-chuck*, I know it's a chipmunk. Its chatter sounds a lot like a cross, chirping bird. It's fun to watch chipmunks. They never stop fussing around—as if they're always looking for something they've lost. They're actually looking for seeds, nuts, or fruit. I never go off and leave my picnic lunch on the ground. Not when a chipmunk is around. If I do, some of my berries or cherries are sure to be gone!

Chipmunks scamper all over the woods, searching for seeds, nuts, and fruit.

Snowshoe hares look a lot like cottontail rabbits. But as soon as one jumps you know it's a hare. A hare can leap several feet in one hop—much farther than a rabbit can jump. The hare's feet are big. They are long, wide, and flat—like snowshoes, I guess. The hare can run fast from an enemy if it has to, especially in winter, on snow. A hare is a weasel's favorite food.

A young snowshoe hare hunkers down on its big, hind feet.

Long-tailed weasels chase and eat many small animals that live in the woods.

A long-tailed weasel could give a hare a good chase—at least on bare ground, if not on snow. In spite of its short little legs, a weasel also runs fast. Its back humps up and down as it bounds over the ground. Its long body is so skinny the weasel can wedge itself into burrows, small holes in logs, and spaces among rocks. Night and day, it hunts for hares, rabbits, chipmunks, rats, mice, voles, even birds. There aren't many animals it can't dig out or outrun.

A bobcat looks like a soft, furry cat—the kind that would lie on your lap and purr. But bobcats are not tame. They hunt, mostly at night, for rats and mice—and especially rabbits and hares. I saw one once, just when the sun was going down. Its stump of a tail stood stiff and straight out behind as it stared hard at the ground. Pretty soon, it stretched, just like my cat does at home—its front legs on the ground, its rear end in the air. Then it disappeared into the shrubs—to stalk something else, I suppose.

A bobcat is about to pounce on a mouse, a rat, a rabbit, or a hare—whatever is there.

A bobcat would not go after a moose! It's the biggest kind of deer in the world. I've heard moose crashing around in the bushes, as if it would tear them all down. And, one time, I saw one in a clear place in the woods. It was a bull moose. Its antlers spread out from its huge, horsy head. The antlers looked to me like two gigantic baseball mitts—wide open, as if they were waiting to catch a big ball.

A male moose crashes out from the shelter of trees to browse in a forest field.

I like to get down on my knees in the woods and pick up a handful of crumbly soil. The forest floor tells stories about what's gone on here before. The soil is nothing like grainy sand on a beach. It's lumpy and thick, and it smells of damp wood. It's full of twigs, pieces of bark, pine needles, and brown, shredded leaves. You find slivers of animal bones, chips of broken eggshells, and feathers of birds. With a fistful of dirt, you can almost feel like you're holding the forest's whole story right there in your hands.

You find bits of wood, bones, feathers, and shells in one handful of damp, forest soil.

More About Forestlands

Black bears

American toads are spotted toads that live in damp places in forests, meadows, and backyards. They usually hunt at night for insects, earthworms, and slugs.

Black bears can grow to be 5 feet (1.5 m) long and usually weigh from 200 to 300 pounds (90 to 140 kg). Most live to be about ten years old.

Bobcats are cats with short "bob" or "knob" tails. They are most active during the night, when they hunt for rodents, rabbits, and other prey.

Chipmunks feed on seeds, plants, snails, slugs, and nuts. They burrow in long, deep tunnels and hibernate in the winter.

Deciduous forests are forests where oaks, maples, beeches, elms, and other leafy trees grow. Their broad, flat leaves drop off in the fall. ("Deciduous" means "falling off.")

Gray tree frogs first live as tadpoles in swamps and ponds. As grown frogs, they eat spiders and small bugs.

Chipmunk

Hemlocks are evergreen trees that grow 60 to 70 feet (18 to 21 m) tall. Seeds lie under the tight-fitting scales of hemlock cones. Their leafy twigs were once used to make tea.

Hummingbirds have tiny wings that beat 55 to 75 times every second. Their name comes from the humming sound of their wings when they fly.

Long-tailed weasels have tails as long as their long, short-legged bodies. Brown northern weasels turn white in the fall—except for the black tip of their tails.

Gray tree frog

Luna moths are among the largest moths in North America. They have long tails and their wingspan is 4.5 to 5.0 inches (11 to 13 cm).

Mixed forests are woodlands where cone-bearing evergreen trees (such as hemlocks, spruces, and firs) grow alongside deciduous trees (such as oaks, birches, maples).

Moose are about the size of horses. Males (bulls) grow to be 6.5 to 7.5 feet (1.95 to 2.25 m) tall. Females (cows) are smaller. Only the bulls grow antlers each year.

Luna moth

Nashville warblers

Nashville warblers are small, migrating (traveling) birds. They nest and raise their young as far north as Canada. They winter as far south as Central America and Costa Rica.

Northern saw-whet owls are small brown owls. The name "saw-whet" comes from the owls' raspy call, like the sound of a saw being whetted (sharpened).

Pileated woodpeckers are the largest of all woodpeckers. They are called "pileated" (which means "capped") because of the red-and-black feathers on top of their heads.

Porcupines are rodents (animals that gnaw). Their quills are sharp bristles of hairs stuck together. New quills grow when old ones are lost.

Puffballs are the fruits (mushrooms) of underground fungi roots. Puffballs can be small as golf balls or big as basketballs. They are also called "smokeballs."

Red squirrels are small, furry animals that live in tree nests or in holes in logs or the ground. They eat and store seeds, acorns and other nuts.

Showy lady's slippers grow in moist soil in woods, swamps, and bogs. They have

Red squirrel

Snowshoe hare

white and pink flowers and are part of the orchid family.

Snowshoe hares have large, furry hind feet and can leap 12 feet (3.5 m) in one bound. Their fur is brown in the summer and white in the winter.

White-tailed deer live in forests throughout North America. Male deer are called bucks, stags, or harts. Female deer are called does or hinds.

Wolf spiders do not weave webs. They hide and grab insects that pass by. They hunt alone—not (as it was once thought) like wolves that hunt in packs.

For More Information

Aronson, Steven M.L. *Trees: Trees Identified by Leaf, Bark and Seed.* New York: Workman, 1998.

Bishop, Nic. *Forest Explorer: A Life-Sized Field Guide.* New York: Scholastic, 2004.

Canizares, Susan. *Evergreens are Green.* New York: Scholastic, 1997.

Hickman, Pamela. *In the Woods.* Halifax NS, Canada: Formac Distributing, 1998.

Kalman, Bobbie and Kathryn Smithyman. *What Is a Forest?* New York: Crabtree, 2002.

Nadeau, Issac. Food Chains in a Forest Habitat. New York: Rosen, 2001.

www.nationalgeographic.com/forest
Life in a deciduous forest.
(Missouri Botanical Garden)

www.panda.org
All kinds of forests: deciduous, coniferous, mixed, and tropical.
(World Wildlife Fund)

Index

antlers, 38, 43

bear, 18–19, 20, 40
bees, 18
birds, 6–9, 21, 30–32, 42, 44
black bear, 18–19, 20, 40
bobcat, 36–37, 40–41
broad–leaf trees, 3

chipmunk, 33, 41
cone–bearing trees, 3, 28–29, 43

deciduous trees, 3, 22–23, 41, 43
deer, 20, 27, 46

evergreen trees, 3, 22–23, 42, 43

flowers, 27, 45–46
frog, 14, 41
fungi, 24, 45

gray tree frog, 14, 41

hare, 34, 37, 46
hemlock tree, 28–29, 42
hummingbird, 8, 21, 42

lady's slippers, 27, 45
leafy forest, 5–21
long–tailed weasel, 35, 42
luna moth, 10–11, 43

mixed forest, 22–39, 43
moose, 38, 43
moth, 10–11, 43
mushrooms, 15, 17, 24–25, 45

Nashville warbler, 30–31, 44

owl, 32, 44

pileated woodpecker, 9, 44
porcupine, 13, 45
puffball mushroom, 15, 17, 45

quills, 13, 45

red squirrels, 12, 45
rodents, 41, 45
ruby–throated hummingbird, 8

saw–whet owl, 32, 44
snowshoe hare, 34, 46
spider, 26, 46
spores, 15, 17
squirrels, 12, 45

toad, 25, 40
tree frog, 14, 41

warbler, 30–31, 44
weasel, 34, 35, 42
white–tailed deer, 20, 46
wolf spider, 26, 46
woodpecker, 9, 44